PUFFIN BOOKS

The Stray

Dick King-Smith served in the Grenadier Guards
during the Second World War, and afterwards
spent twenty years as a farmer in Gloucestershire,
the county of his birth. Many of his stories are
inspired by his farming experiences. Later he
taught at a village primary school. His first book,
The Fox Busters, was published in 1978. Since then
he has written a great number of children's books,
including *The Sheep-Pig* (winner of the *Guardian*
Award), *Harry's Mad, Noah's Brother, The Hodgeheg,
Martin's Mice, Ace, The Cuckoo Child, Harriet's Hare*
(winner of the Children's Book Award in 1995)
and many others. At the British Book Awards in
1992 he was voted Children's Author of the Year.
He is married, with three children and ten
grandchildren, and lives in a seventeenth Century
cottage a short crow's-flight from the house where
he was born.

Dick King-Smith
The
STRAY

Illustrated by Frank Rodgers

PUFFIN BOOKS

PUFFIN BOOKS

Published by the Penguin Group
Penguin Books Ltd, 27 Wrights Lane, London W8 5TZ, England
Penguin Books USA Inc., 375 Hudson Street, New York, New York 10014, USA
Penguin Books Australia Ltd, Ringwood, Victoria, Australia
Penguin Books Canada Ltd, 10 Alcorn Avenue, Toronto, Ontario, Canada M4V 3B2
Penguin Books (NZ) Ltd, 182–190 Wairau Road, Auckland 10, New Zealand

Penguin Books Ltd, Registered Offices: Harmondsworth, Middlesex, England

First published by Viking 1997
Published in Puffin Books 1997
7 9 10 8

Text copyright © Fox Busters Ltd, 1997
Illustrations copyright © Frank Rodgers, 1997
All rights reserved

The moral right of the author has been asserted

Filmset in Palatino

Made and printed in England by Clays Ltd, St Ives plc

British Library Cataloguing in Publication Data
A CIP catalogue record for this book is available from the British Library

ISBN 0–140–38142–2

Contents

One	Escaping	1
Two	Arriving	14
Three	Staying	25
Four	Picnicking	36
Five	Aching	46
Six	Bombing	56
Seven	Gambling	65
Eight	Rescuing	73
Nine	Ailing	80
Ten	Wishing	92
Eleven	Adopting	102
Twelve	Worrying	112
Thirteen	Winning	123
Fourteen	Remembering	131

Chapter One

Escaping

Early one morning Henny Hickathrift awoke with her mind made up. That very day she would run away from home.

To be more accurate, she would run away from *the* Home, the Old People's Home where she lived.

I'm bored, she said to herself. I'm bored with this boring place and all the boring old people who live in it, and I'm not stopping here a moment longer.

So she got dressed, and packed up her very few possessions in a little suitcase, and wrote a note which she left on her pillow.

It said:

Gone to stay with my sister in Birmingham.

And she signed it:

Henrietta Hickathrift

Not only had Henny no sister in Birmingham, she had no sister at all, or brother, or other living relative. Her mother and father had died ages ago, for Henny was seventy-five years old.

Now, suitcase in one hand, walking-stick in the other, she sneaked out of the Old People's Home, making sure that no one saw her leave, and set off down the road.

It was a lovely sunny summer's morning, just right for running away, and Henny was so much enjoying her new-found freedom that she walked happily along without really thinking where she was going.

But after a while the suitcase began to feel rather heavy and her feet a bit sore, so she sat down on a park bench for a little rest. Nearby, some children were playing with a football, which presently rolled across the path and hit Henny Hickathrift, quite gently, on the legs.

A boy came running up.

'Sorry,' he said. 'You all right?'

'Fine, thanks,' said Henny. 'I'm running away from home.'

'Oh,' said the boy. 'Where are you going to?'

Where *am* I going? thought Henny. I know!

'To the seaside,' she said.

'Oh,' said the boy. 'That will be nice.' And he picked up the football and ran off.

'It will,' said Henny out loud. 'I haven't been to the seaside since I was a girl, and the weather's lovely, and I've still got quite a bit of my pension money left, so why don't I go by train? I haven't been on a train for ages either.'

Off she set again, and found her way to the railway station. There, the first thing she saw was a big coloured poster stuck on the wall. It showed a picture of a happy family on the beach, the mother and father relaxing in deckchairs, watching the children building a big sandcastle. The sands were golden, and in the brilliantly blue sky flew snow-white gulls.

Come to *sunny* SALTMOUTH!

it said.

'I will,' said Henny.

She went to the ticket office.

'A single ticket to Saltmouth, please,' she said. 'Third Class.'

The ticket clerk peered out of his window. He saw a little old lady wearing an overcoat that had seen better days and a woollen hat like a tea-cosy on top of her short grey hair.

'There's no such thing as Third Class nowadays,' he said with a sniff. 'It's either First or Standard Class.'

4

'Oh,' said Henny. 'How much is it?'

'Do you have a Senior Citizen's Railcard?'

'No.'

'In that case a Standard Class single ticket to Saltmouth is thirty-two pounds fifty.'

'That's a lot of money,' said Henny.

'It's a long way,' said the clerk shortly. He drummed on the window-ledge with his finger-tips, anxious to be rid of this customer, and looked over her head as though she were delaying a long queue of people, though in fact there was no one behind her.

How rude he is, thought Henny. In the old days he'd have called me Madam, with a smile perhaps, and anyway I don't like people who can't look you in the eye.

She took out her purse. There was fifty pounds in it.

'How much is it First Class?' she said.

'First Class?' said the clerk in a voice which seemed to express amazement that such a person could even contemplate travelling thus.

'Yes. That's what I asked.'

'Forty-five pounds.'

Henrietta Hickathrift remembered a favourite saying of her mother's. Might as well be hanged for a sheep as a lamb, she thought, and she drew

5

herself up to her full height of five feet and one inch and said, 'Kindly give me a First Class ticket.'

The train for Saltmouth was not due for half an hour, so Henny went into the station buffet and bought herself a cup of coffee (which cost her a pound out of the five she had left). Then she sat and waited with excitement for the train to come puffing into the station. But when it arrived, it didn't puff at all, it just hummed. There was no hiss of steam, no plume of smoke coming from the funnel of the locomotive, no funnel indeed.

Henny clambered aboard and found herself a seat in a First Class compartment. How different it was from the last time she had travelled by train. There was no corridor in the long open carriage, just a door at each end that opened in front of you as if by magic, and the windows were huge, and the seats so comfy, and, my, how fast they were going! Henny sat with her stick and her suitcase beside her – the compartment was almost empty – and watched the countryside flashing past at a tremendous speed, and thought of all the old people at the Home, slumped in their chairs watching telly and arguing about which channel they should have on.

Poor old things, she said to herself. I can't think how I stuck it so long. And because she felt so happy to be out of the place, and so comfortable in these First Class surroundings, and a bit tired, she shut her eyes and went to sleep.

She was woken by a deep voice.

'Tickets, please,' it said.

The ticket collector was a large man and Henny was glad to see that he was looking her straight in the eye, and smiling, which showed a lot of teeth. 'Sorry to wake you, ma'am,' he said in a voice like warm treacle.

Henny smiled back and handed him her ticket.

'I'm running away from home,' she said. 'I'm going to the seaside.'

'Glad to hear it, ma'am,' said the collector. 'You'll get nice and brown, this weather.' And he went on his way, rumbling with laughter.

After he had gone, Henny suddenly realized that she was very hungry. She had heard an announcement, saying that there was 'a buffet car situated to the rear of the First Class compartments', and now she thought, it's ten o'clock and I haven't had any breakfast.

She went along and stood behind the counter and looked at all the different sorts of food and drink that were on sale. She thought of the usual boring breakfast that the old people at the Home would have had, and decided she would have

things she really liked. 'In for a penny, in for a pound' was another of her mother's sayings, and she still had four pound coins left.

'I'll have one of those Danish pastries, please,' she said, 'and a prawn-and-mayonnaise sandwich, and a Mars Bar.'

'Anything to drink?' said the steward. 'Tea? Coffee?'

'I think I'll have a Coca Cola,' said Henny. 'I've never tried one of those before. Oh, and I'd better have a tube of fruit gums.'

The steward looked curiously at this little old lady with the tea-cosy hat who had ordered such a strange breakfast.

'You see, I'm going to the seaside,' said Henny. 'I'm running away from home.'

The steward raised his eyebrows.

'Fancy!' he said. 'That'll be three pounds ninety-nine altogether, please.'

After she had finished – and much enjoyed – her meal, Henny settled back in her comfortable First Class seat and went to sleep again. So soundly did she sleep that when she woke, it was to find that it was midday and that the train had arrived at Saltmouth.

Walking-stick in hand, carrying her little suitcase, Henrietta Hickathrift made her way out of the station and set off along a road that was signposted TO THE BEACH. In the pocket of her old overcoat was her purse, and in the purse was her total worldly wealth – one penny.

She spent all that afternoon on the Saltmouth sands. They were just as golden as they had been in the poster and the sky as blue and the gulls as white, and there were children building sand-castles and mums and dads relaxing in deck-chairs. Henny couldn't afford one of those, so she sat instead on her suitcase, and watched the waves breaking and the sun glinting on the water and ate several of her fruit gums and was as happy as a sandboy. Not until much later did she begin to think about what to do next.

She looked around and saw that the beach was almost empty, for the families had all gone back to their hotels or their boarding-houses for their evening meal. Only a few people were still walk-ing along the sands, and the sea was much nearer to her now because the tide was coming in.

Near to her, a solitary thin mongrel dog was nosing about, searching for scraps of food. It wore no collar and did not seem to belong to anyone.

It's a stray, Henny thought, that has no home. Like me. I've run away from mine. She popped the last of the fruit gums in her mouth, and then she picked up her walking-stick, smiling to herself. With the point of it, she wrote on the sand in large letters

I AM A STRAY OLD WOMAN

Then she picked up her suitcase, and made her way up the beach and climbed the long flight of steps that led to the Esplanade high above. At the top she stopped to rest, leaning against the iron railings that flanked the road, and looked down to the sands below.

The beach was empty now and even the dog had gone. All that remained to be seen was her message, towards which the tide was now creeping. As Henny waited to see her words washed out, she heard voices close by.

'Look!' said one.

'What is it?' said another.

'Where?' said other voices.

'There,' said the first voice.

Near Henny five children stood at the railings. They were all of different sizes, ranging from a tall girl to a small boy, but they all had red hair, and they were all gazing down at the message far below.

'What does it say?' asked the smallest, and the tallest read it out to him.

Then they all watched in silence until the waves reached the writing and drowned it.

'How sad,' said the tall girl quietly. 'I wonder who wrote that.'

'I did, actually,' said Henny.

The five red-headed children turned and stared at her in solemn silence.

'I had better introduce myself,' she said. 'My name is Henrietta Hickathrift.'

'We are called Good,' said the tall girl. 'I am Angela, and these are my sisters Eleanor and Rosie and my brothers Barney and Rowley.'

'And you're all here for your holidays?' said Henny.

'No,' said Angela. 'We live in the town.'

'Rowley Good, Ivy Cottage, St Edmund's Street, Saltmouth,' chanted the smallest, as he had been taught to do in case of getting lost. Then he said, 'And where do you live?'

'Well, nowhere, actually,' said Henny. 'You see, I've run away from home.'

'Why? Were you unhappy?' said Rowley.

'Yes.'

'Well, where are you going to sleep tonight?' asked the tall girl Angela.

'I don't know.'

'I do,' said Angela. 'Barney, take Miss Hickathrift's suitcase. Eleanor, Rosie, hold Rowley's hands while we cross the road.' And then, turning to Henny, she said, 'Would you like to follow us?'

A friend in need is a friend indeed, thought Henny, as mother would have said, let alone five friends, and she did as she was asked.

Five minutes later the procession arrived outside a long low white house that overlooked the harbour with its rows of moored boats, and Angela knocked upon the front door.

As it opened, she said, 'Mum, we've brought a lady home with us.'

'She's got nowhere to sleep tonight, Mum,' said Barney and Eleanor and Rosie.

'She's a stray,' said Rowley.

Chapter Two
Arriving

Ivy Cottage was one of the oldest houses in the
seaside resort of Saltmouth. Long ago, when the
town had been no more than a fishing village,
there had been three cottages, fishermen's
homes, that had later been knocked together.
And now, because it was long and low and
whitewashed, and had its own small lawn that
ran down before it to the sea-wall, it looked
like a country home, in contrast to the tall
Victorian buildings that stood behind and to
either side of it.

Henny Hickathrift didn't notice any of this at the time of course. Partly she was a bit tired after her long journey, partly a little dazed from sitting in the sun, but mostly she felt herself to be in a dreamlike state, happy to follow these red-haired children wherever they should go.

Now she saw, in the doorway of Ivy Cottage, a tall fair-haired woman, and said, as she often did, the first thing that came into her head.

'They don't get it from you then?' she remarked.

Mrs Good smiled, looking, Henny was glad to see, very directly at her, and said, 'The hair, you mean?'

'Yes.'

'No, that comes from my husband's side of the family.'

'Is he red-haired?'

'Well, more grey now, what's left of it.'

'My mother,' said Henny, 'used to tell me that red-headed men were either Irish or bad-tempered or both.'

The children's mother laughed.

'Not this one,' she said. 'He's English and pretty even-tempered. But do come in . . .' she paused and glanced at Henny's left hand and saw no rings, 'Miss . . .' She paused again.

'Hickathrift,' said Henny. 'Henrietta Hickathrift.'

'I'm Mary Good. Do come in, and Angela, would you put the kettle on? I'm sure Miss Hickathrift would like a cup of tea.'

'Please call me Henny. Everybody does,' said Henny.

'Can we call you Henny?' said Rowley.

'I don't think . . .' began his mother.

'Of course you can,' said Henny. 'Because I'll tell you a secret. I'm one of those funny people that actually likes children.'

'How many children have you got?' asked Rowley.

'I'm sorry,' said Mary Good quickly. 'He's only four, and . . .'

'No, don't worry,' said Henny, and to Rowley she said, 'I never had any children, worse luck. You see, I never married. A long time ago, during the Second World War, I was engaged to be married, to a soldier, but he was killed, and after that I never wanted to marry anyone else.'

Angela came in with the tea things, including a plate of biscuits, just in time to hear this. She looked sad, as did Eleanor and Rosie.

Barney looked interested, because he was doing a school project on the Second World War and wanted to ask questions about this long-dead soldier – what regiment was he in, what was his rank, in what battle did he die? – but didn't like to.

Rowley only said, 'Can I have a biscuit?'

'Funny to think,' said Henny to the children, 'that if I had had a daughter, she'd have been about the same age as your mum, I imagine.' And to Mary Good she said, 'Tell me how old all these people are.'

'Well, like I said, Rowley's four, nearly five, and Rosie is seven, and Eleanor's nine, and Barney is eleven, and Angela is thirteen. Milk? Sugar?'

'Both, please,' said Henny.

'Will you have a biscuit?' said Angela. 'They're Garibaldis.'

'Ooh, "squashed flies"!' said Henny. 'I've always loved those, ever since I was very young.'

'How old are you now?' said Rowley.

'Rowley!' said everyone, but Henny only smiled at him and said, 'As old as my tongue and a little older than my teeth.'

'Dad knows all about them,' said Rowley. 'He's a dentist, Dad is. Can I have another biscuit, Mum?'

'He's had three already!' said several voices, and Rowley's mother said, 'No, you can't,' and Henny said, 'Actually, if you really want to know, Rowley, I'm seventy-five years old. Today.'

'Today?' cried everyone. 'It's your birthday?'

'Yes. I woke up early this morning and I thought – well, old girl, no one's going to give you a birthday present so you might as well give yourself one. So I did. I ran away. That was my present to myself.'

'Because you were unhappy, Henny,' said the tall girl Angela. 'That's what you told us.'

18

'Yes. You see, I've been living in an Old People's Home and I don't really feel like an Old Person and it certainly didn't feel like Home. Mind you, I did think of a couple of things my mother used to say. One was "Look before you leap" and another was "There's no fool like an old fool." But then yet another one was "There's no time like the present." So I scarpered.'

'And now you've burned your boats,' said Mary Good.

'Yes, just what Mother would have said. And now I really must be going. Thank you for the tea and the squashed flies – you've been very kind.'

'Just a moment,' said Mary Good. 'I understood the children to say that you had nowhere to sleep tonight?'

'I expect I'll find somewhere,' said Henny.

'You already have.'

Henny looked at Mary Good and saw that she was smiling. People smile for different reasons and in different ways. This, Henny thought, was a specially nice smile, warm and welcoming.

'Are you offering me a bed for the night?' she said.

'I am.'

'It's very kind of you, Mrs Good . . .'

'Mary.'

'. . . Mary. But the fact is, I couldn't possibly afford it,' said Henny. 'You see, I've used up all my money, running away. To tell you the truth, all I've got left is one penny.'

'Listen, Henny,' said Mary Good. 'We all heard you say just now that no one was going to give you a birthday present. Well, you were wrong. We're going to give you one. We'll find you somewhere to sleep tonight, and I'll tell you what, children – let's give Henny a birthday feast, to celebrate.'

'Can we help with it?' said Angela and Barney and Eleanor and Rosie.

'Can we have ice-cream?' said Rowley.

When the children's father arrived home from his dental surgery and walked into the sitting-room of Ivy Cottage, neither his wife nor any of his five children were there (since they were all busy in the kitchen). Instead he saw a little old lady sitting in one of the armchairs.

'Hullo!' he said. 'Where have you sprung from?'

'From an Old People's Home, actually,' said Henny. 'I ran away.'

She looked up at this large man: what hair he had left was reddish, she saw, tinged with grey.

'So, you're not Irish,' she said.

The dentist shook his head in bewilderment.

'No,' he said.

'Or bad-tempered.'

At this point Rowley came in, carrying a Pyrex bowl which he was scraping out with a spoon.

'They made the pudding in this,' he said. 'D'you want a lick, Henny?'

Taking advantage of this diversion, his father dodged out of the room and went in search of his wife.

'Mary,' he said. 'What on earth is happening? There's a strange old woman in the sitting-room, talking a lot of nonsense. Is she mad?'

'No, George, not in the slightest,' said his wife.

'She's called Henrietta Hickathrift, Dad,' said Angela, 'and we're giving her a birthday party.'

'And she was going to marry a soldier,' said Barney, 'but he got killed.'

'And she's only got one penny in the world,' said Eleanor.

'And,' said Rosie, 'she likes squashed flies.'

'It must be me that's gone mad,' said George Good. 'I think I need a drink.'

'Ask Henny what she'd like,' said his wife.

Going back to the sitting-room, he found Rowley deep in conversation with the old lady.

'Can you swim, Henny?' Rowley was saying.

'Yes. Though I haven't for ages.'

'I can, with armbands. I'm going to be an Olympic swimmer probably and win a gold medal, I expect.'

'Um, Miss, um, Hickathrift,' said George Good. 'May I offer you something to drink?'

'Call her Henny, Dad,' said Rowley. 'Everybody does.'

'Do you have any Coca Cola?' said Henny.

'Can I have some, Dad?' said Rowley.

'Nothing stronger?' said his father to Henny.

'Oh no, thank you. I had some for my breakfast and I thought it very strong. In fact it sent me straight to sleep. It's a good job that nice ticket collector came along before breakfast – he'd have had a job to wake me, I dare say. You'd have been interested in his teeth. Lots of them.'

'Really?' said the dentist. 'I think I'll have a little whisky,' and he poured himself a large one.

'Rowley,' he said. 'Run out to the kitchen and see what Mum would like and if the others want Coke too.' And then he handed Henny her glass and raised his own.

'Well, cheers!' he said.

Henny did not recall her late father's sayings in the way that she remembered her mother's, perhaps because he had been a man who never said much. But it came to her at that moment what he always said when he had a drink.

'Here's mud in your eye!' she replied.

George Good took a large gulp of whisky.

'Your first visit to Saltmouth?' he asked.

'Yes.'

'And where are you staying?'

'Here,' said Henny.

Chapter Three
Staying

Raiding her deep-freeze, Mary Good had contrived a slap-up meal. There was even a cake with H.H. on it in silver bobbles, and seven and a half candles (one for each ten years and a half-candle for the extra five), and everyone sang, 'Happy birthday, dear Henny, happy birthday to you,' the children very loudly, as though they had known her all their lives.

Ivy Cottage – because it had originally been three dwellings – had a good number of bedrooms. Not till the children were all in theirs and the stray had also gone to bed did George Good have a chance to speak to his wife about their surprise visitor.

'Look, Mary,' he said, 'I quite see that you couldn't turn the old girl away, but presumably she will find somewhere to go tomorrow? I mean, she's quite a character, I can see that, and the children seem almost to have adopted her already – it's Henny this and Henny that all the time – but if we're not careful, we shall have a job to shift her, now she's got her feet under the table. You'll be saying, "Just for one more night, just for a week," and so on, I know you, you're too soft-hearted.'

'All right, George,' said Mary Good. 'We'll let her have a good night's sleep, and then tomorrow you can throw her out.'

'Throw her out? Me?'

'Yes, I'm not going to. Not yet, anyway.'

One of the spare bedrooms at Ivy Cottage was part of an extension that had been built on to the end. The lower part was a double garage, and above was one small bedroom with its own little bathroom. A flight of outside wooden steps with a handrail led up to it. The family called it 'the flat'.

Next morning Angela climbed these steps with a cup of tea and knocked on the bedroom door. There was no answer, even when she knocked again – loudly – and called 'Henny!'

Awful thoughts ran through Angela's mind. Had yesterday been too much for the runaway, at her age? Was the birthday to be followed by the deathday?

She peeped in. The room was empty. But then she saw that the little suitcase was still there, as well as the tea-cosy hat. But no walking-stick.

Angela dashed down the steps again and ran down across the lawn to look over the sea-wall. In the harbour below a few boatmen were messing about, doing whatever it is that people do to their boats, but then Angela saw, on the sand beyond, a small grey-haired figure trudging along.

'Henny!' shouted Angela, waving, and the figure waved back with her walking-stick.

'Where have you been?' said Angela when they met.

'For a nice walk,' said Henny. 'The seagulls woke me up, sitting on the roof above, cackling, and I looked out and saw what a lovely morning it was, so off I went. Did you think I'd run away again?'

Angela didn't say what she had thought. Instead she said, 'You won't, will you?'

'Well, I'll have to go somewhere,' said Henny.

'Why?'

'Because your mum and dad don't want to be landed with a penniless stranger.'

'You're not a stranger,' said Angela. 'I feel as if I've known you for an awfully long time. And you're not penniless – you've got one left – and

28

anyway I've got some money saved that you can have, and we were talking yesterday evening and the others all said they'd give you some of their pocket money. Except Rowley. He said he couldn't afford to give any of his but he'd lend you fifty p.'

'You're all very kind,' said Henny. 'Good by name, good by nature.'

After breakfast George Good rose from the table, saying, 'Have a lovely day then, you lot. You're lucky, you are, all on your holidays in this lovely weather, while I'm stuck indoors, peering into people's mouths.'

'George,' said his wife. 'Didn't you have something to say to Henny?'

'To Henny? Oh. No, no, I don't think so.'

'Adieu, perhaps?'

'Adieu? No, no, it seems that it would be more correct to say "Au revoir",' said the dentist, and, suppressing a sigh, set off to walk to his surgery.

'Was that French?' asked Rowley.

'Yes,' said the others.

'I know some French,' he said.

'What?'

'Bong jooer.'

'Bong jooer,' they all replied.

'Can you clear the table, children,' their mother said, 'and do the washing-up between you? I want to have a quiet chat with Henny.'

'Can I have a quiet chat too?' said Rowley.

'No.'

'OK,' said Rowley. 'O rev wah.'

Once they were sitting comfortably in armchairs and the cat had chosen Henny's lap to settle himself upon, Mary Good said, 'Now tell me, what are your plans? I mean, have you thought better of this running-away business? Wouldn't it be more sensible to treat it all as just an outing, and go back to your Old People's Home? We'd see to your train fare, you don't need to worry about that. It's not that I imagine it's much fun living in a place like that, but presumably they look after you quite well, and then there's your pension book, they must have that. Oughtn't you to go back?'

'Never,' said Henny.

'What will you do then?'

'Well, Mary,' said Henny, 'I know what I'd like to do. I'd like to stay in Saltmouth. It's all been so wonderful – yesterday afternoon, sitting on the sands, and then that marvellous supper you made, and going up the steps to that lovely little flat – like a child climbing into a tree-house – and having a room to myself: at the Home I had to share with a couple of other old ducks that snored and quacked in their sleep. Oh, I haven't felt so carefree since I was Angela's age.'

'Have you not had a happy life then, Henny?' asked Mary Good.

'Mustn't complain, I suppose,' said Henny, 'but I spent most of it looking after my parents. Mother was a bit of an invalid and Father never did a lot, so I stayed home and kept house for them. Housework! Well, you'd know all about that, in a big place like this. Cooking for seven, to start with. That must take up a lot of your time.'

'Yes, but I like cooking. It's my hobby, I suppose.'

'What about all the dusting and cleaning?'

'Oh, I don't like that.'

'Sewing? Mending?'

'I'm hopeless at that.'

'Ironing?'

'Ugh! Horrible.'

'Polishing the brass and the silver? Getting between the tines of all the forks?'

'Oh stop it, Henny!' cried Mary Good. 'I hate all those jobs. Of course very few people employ servants nowadays, but I remember that my grandparents had a living-in servant to do all those sorts of things, a housemaid.'

'Mary,' said Henny. 'I may not be as young as I was, but I can still do all those sorts of things. How would *you* like to have a housemaid?'

'She said *what*?' cried George Good when he came home for his lunch. Henny and the five children had all gone down to the beach, taking a picnic.

'"How would you like to have a housemaid?"' said Mary Good. 'Those were her words.'

'I was right,' said her husband. 'She *is* mad. How can anyone suddenly become a domestic servant at the age of seventy-five? She couldn't possibly do the work. Anyway, we don't need to employ anyone, you've always managed perfectly well on your own, haven't you?'

'Yes.'

'And you've always said you don't want a strange woman in your house?'

'Yes.'

'Well, Henny's strange enough, I should have thought. Don't tell me you're actually thinking of agreeing to this hare-brained idea?'

'I'd like you to consider it, George,' said his wife.

'Consider it? I consider it crazy. Where's she going to live, for starters?'

'In the flat.'

'In the flat? What about when your parents come to visit? Or mine?'

'That little room with a single bed is no use to either lot of grandparents, you know that. They always go in the big spare room.'

'But think of the value of that flat. Here, in Saltmouth, in the season, we could let that to someone for a lot of money.'

'But we don't want to, do we?'

'Yet you want that old woman to live in it. Rent free, I suppose? And what about the expense of her wages, when she starts playing at being a housemaid?'

'Henny will write to the Home and ask them to forward her pension book, explaining that she is staying with friends indefinitely.'

'Friends? Indefinitely?'

'And then each week we will take some of her pension for her bed and board and she'll keep the rest for her spending money. Just think of it, George, from my point of view. No more ironing, no more silver-cleaning, no more mending the children's clothes or sewing on buttons – all things that a fit seventy-five-year-old can easily do. And a permanent sitter-in whenever we want to go out in the evenings. Don't you think we should give the idea a try? Just for a month, say?'

34

'I knew it, I knew it!' said George Good. 'I told you so, didn't I? I said that's what you'd say – "just for a night, just for a week" – and now it's "just for a month". You and your soft heart. You must be soft in the head too. Quite apart from the pros and cons of this mad scheme, we don't know anything at all about Miss Henrietta Hickathrift.'

'I like her,' said Mary Good. 'I like her very well. And the children think she's marvellous. But of course if you say No to the idea, then No it must be.'

The dentist shook his bald head irritably, like a cornered bull.

'I haven't said No,' he replied.

'That makes things much easier,' said his wife before he could continue, 'because I've already said Yes.'

Chapter Four
Picnicking

On the beach, Henny and the Good children were picnicking. They had gone down early, to make sure of their favourite spot before any holiday-makers should get it.

It was in a narrow triangular cleft between two big rocks at the base of the cliffs. Once they had parked themselves there, no one else could get in, and they thought of this little patch of sand with its rocky walls as a kind of second home. At the back of it there was actually a small cave, in which, if it rained, they could seek cover.

The children would strew their belongings around and drape their towels on the rocks and, when they went down to the beach to play or to bathe, they would barricade the entrance to their chosen place with spades and buckets. Barney had made a notice board out of cardboard with strings attached so that it could be hung on a spade, and had let Rowley write the notice with a big red felt pen. It said:

KEP OUT

This morning the children had been swimming already. Angela was a strong swimmer, ready to act as lifeguard if anyone needed help. Barney swam well, Eleanor quite well, Rosie a bit, and Rowley sploshed about with his armbands on. Henny took off her shoes and stockings, rolled up her skirt, and paddled.

Now everyone was very hungry, so they decided to have the picnic early. The Goods' picnics were always the same – sandwiches and fruit.

Each child had an apple and a banana, but the sandwiches varied from picnic to picnic, according to whose turn it was to choose what should be in them.

If it was Angela's, for example, she always chose cheese, and so then they all had cheese sandwiches. Barney always chose peanut butter, Eleanor Marmite, Rosie strawberry jam, and Rowley Golden Syrup sandwiches. On this day it had actually been Eleanor's turn.

'So it's Marmite,' said her mother.

'No,' said Eleanor.

'You want a change? You always have Marmite.'

'No. Let Henny choose,' said Eleanor.

'Good girl,' her mother said. 'Henny, what's your favourite sandwich?'

'Oh, I don't think I'd better tell you,' said Henny. 'They'd be too much trouble to make and the children might not like them. No, I'd better not say.'

'Oh, go on, Henny!' they all cried.

'Well, it's prawn-and-mayonnaise. I had one on the train coming here, it was delicious.'

'No trouble,' said Mary Good, 'and I'm sure the children will like them.'

'I shan't,' said Rowley.

But when it came to it, he bolted his sandwiches like a wolf.

'Nice, Rowley?' said Henny.

'All right.'

'Nicer than Golden Syrup?' asked Rosie.

'He would probably have liked a prawn-and-mayonnaise-and-Golden-Syrup sandwich,' said Barney.

'I would,' said Rowley. 'Can I have an ice-cream now?'

No one answered.

Further along the beach there was a little café that sold ice-creams, and when the children's parents were there, they could usually be persuaded to treat them. Rowley in particular considered that grown-ups had a duty to provide ice-creams.

'Can I, Henny?' he said again. 'Please?'

'Who's going to pay for it?' said Henny.

'You are.'

'I've only got a penny.'

'And I haven't brought any money with me,' said Angela.

'Nor me,' said the other three.

Rowley sighed, shaking his head.

'You know, Henny, you'll have to earn some money,' he said. 'You'll have to get a job,' and he took the KEP OUT notice off his spade and went to dig a hole.

'As a matter of fact,' said Henny to the others, 'I've got one. I got it this morning, before we came down to the beach.'

'That's wonderful!' said Angela. 'What job have you got?'

'Housemaid.'

'Housemaid?' they cried. 'What does that mean? What will you have to do?'

'Oh, some cleaning, some ironing, some mending, that sort of thing.'

'But where?'

'Here in Saltmouth.'

'Whereabouts in Saltmouth?'

'Place called Ivy Cottage.'

There was a pause of perhaps three seconds while this sank in, before the four older children let out a whoop of delight.

'That's marvellous!' said Angela.

'That's great!' said Barney.

'Ace!' said Eleanor.

'Brill!' said Rosie.

Rowley, busy digging, had not properly understood.

'I just wish I could have an ice-cream,' he kept muttering.

'And so you shall,' said Henny. 'Angela, where's the nearest place that sells them?'

'There's a café,' said Angela. 'Over there. But Henny, you haven't any money.'

'Don't worry about that,' said Henny. 'You just stay here and look after the others. I won't be long.'

As she walked along the beach, Henny remembered another of her mother's many sayings – honesty is the best policy – and when she reached the café, she said to the owner, 'I want six large ice-cream cornets, please, but I think I should warn you that this is all the money I have,' and she took from her purse that last penny and put it on the counter.

The man stared at her (very directly, Henny noted).

'Are you asking me,' he said, 'to give you three pounds' worth of ice-cream for a penny?'

'Yes,' said Henny.

She unstrapped her wrist-watch and handed it to him.

'You keep this,' she said, 'till I can pay you. It's old but reliable, like me. I have an honest face, wouldn't you say?'

The man looked more closely still at this odd little grey-haired woman, and thought – as people

41

often did of Henrietta Hickathrift – that he had seldom seen such an open, friendly and patently honest face as this.

'Which flavour would you like, madam?' he said.

'Strawberry!' shouted Rowley when Henny arrived back, three pink cornets in each hand. 'Lush!'

'But how. . . ?' began Angela.

Henny winked at her.

'Ask me no questions,' she said, 'and I'll tell you no lies. As mother used to say.'

Rowley took a long lick of his ice-cream.

'How old's your mother, Henny?' he said.

'She'd be a hundred this year,' said Henny, 'if she was still alive.'

'Dead, is she?' said Rowley.

'Yes. She died years and years ago. So did my father. I'm not just a stray, I'm an orphan too!'

'But you're not a stray any more, Henny,' said Angela. 'Now that you're going to live with us.'

Rowley pricked up his ears.

'Are you?' he said.

'Yes.'

'In the flat?'

'Yes.'

'Good,' said Rowley happily. 'Then you can buy ice-creams every day.'

He took another long slobbery lick.

'Too many sweet things are bad for your teeth,' said Henny.

'Dad's always telling us that,' said Barney.

'You're lucky, having a dentist for a father,' said Henny. 'I bet you've all got wonderful teeth.'

'We have,' said Eleanor.

'Look,' said Rosie, and she drew back her lips and bared her teeth at Henny, and then the rest did the same.

'Show us yours, Henny,' said Rowley.

'No fear,' said Henny. 'Mine are ugly old yellow things, those I've got left. I never took proper care of them when I was young.'

'Why not?' asked Eleanor.

'Terrified of the dentist.'

'Are you frightened of Dad then?' asked Rosie.

'I would be if I was sitting in his dentist's chair.'

'He's ever so gentle,' said Barney. 'He never hurts us a bit.'

'That's because you've all got perfect teeth that don't need anything doing to them. I bet he'd hurt me.'

'Well, what do you do if you get toothache?' asked Angela.

'Grin and bear it,' said Henny.

She took a mouthful of her ice-cream.

'Ooh, it's cold!' she said.

Then suddenly she gave a little jump and clapped a hand to her cheek.

'Ow!' she cried.

Chapter Five

Aching

Oh! said Henny quietly to herself for the umpteenth time. Twenty-four hours had gone but the toothache hadn't.

She had begged some aspirins from Mary Good, saying she had a headache, but they hadn't helped. As usual, one of the late Mrs Hickathrift's many sayings came to mind – 'What can't be cured must be endured' – but the sudden shooting pain in a big back tooth was now even more frequent.

Nonetheless Henny determined to begin her duties at Ivy Cottage, hoping that work would take her mind off her troubles. She had persuaded the children's mother to go down to the beach with them (Marmite sandwiches, Eleanor's turn now) and was tackling a huge pile of ironing.

When it felt like eleven, she felt like a cup of tea, and looked at her wrist, only to remember where her watch now was; and when she'd made the tea, the first sip of it made her tooth jump like anything.

In fact by the time George Good came home for his lunch, Henny hardly knew what to do with herself, so constant was the sharp nagging pain. But I mustn't show it, she thought. She remembered her last visit to a dentist, half a lifetime ago, especially the awful buzzing of the drill inside her mouth.

'All alone then?' said today's dentist.

'Yes, they've all gone down to the beach. I've put your lunch all ready.'

'Aren't you going to have some?'

'No, I don't feel like eating, thank you.'

'You're not ill?'

'No, no, I'm fine,' said Henny, and at that

instant the pain stabbed at her, viciously, as though to punish her for telling such a whopper.

'Oh! Oh!' she cried, clapping both hands on one side of her face.

'I don't have to be a dentist,' said George Good, 'to tell that you have the toothache. Haven't you?'

Henny nodded.

'Well, you've come to the right shop. As it happens, I've got a cancellation this afternoon. I can fit you in.'

Henny shook her head.

'No? Why not?'

'I'm terrified of going to the dentist. I always have been.'

'When did you last have your teeth checked?'

'About thirty years ago,' said Henny. 'I shall never forget it. Oh, that awful drill. I can hear it now. And I had to have two out as well, and he gave me gas, it was so nasty, the smell of it, and I went all woozy and I could hear sort of Chinese music inside my head, oh, it was all so horrible!'

'Look, Henny,' said George Good, 'things are different these days. I wouldn't dream of giving you gas, and I promise you I shan't hurt you at all. The worst you'll have to put up with may be a little injection of a local anaesthetic, a tiny pinprick, you won't even feel it.'

'I don't believe you.'

'Try it and see.'

'No. Anyway, I can't afford it.'

'Don't worry about that, let's do something about that toothache.'

'It may go away.'

'And it may not. Now, do you know where my surgery is? It's not far.'

'Yes, we walked past it yesterday on our way to the beach. Angela pointed it out to me. I shuddered, just looking at it.'

George Good smiled.

'I've seen lots of frightened patients in my time,' he said, 'but they're all pleasantly surprised in the end. You be down at the surgery at three thirty.'

Henny grasped at one last straw.

'I can't,' she said. 'I can't leave the house until the others come back.'

'That's easily fixed,' said the dentist. 'We'll use the Patent Good Emergency Recall Method. Come and watch.'

Henny followed him as, armed with a pair of binoculars and a large whistle, he walked down the Ivy Cottage lawn to the sea-wall.

First, he raised the binoculars and scanned the beach.

'Right, they're in our usual spot,' he said.

Then he put the whistle to his mouth and blew seven loud blasts,

'Peep – pip – pip – peep – peep! Peep! Peep!'

Quite a number of holidaymakers, Henny could see, turned their heads at this noise, but then, seeing nothing out of the ordinary, lost interest in what it might mean. But from the cleft in the rocks a figure came out and began to run along the beach towards the harbour. It was Barney. He ran up the ramp that led to the harbour and then along the jetty, until he stood, panting, directly below them.

'What's the matter, Dad?' he called up.

His father leaned over the wall.

'Ask Mum if she'll have you all back here by three fifteen will you?'

'Why?'

'Henny has an appointment with me at three thirty. OK?'

'OK,' said Barney.

'OK?' said his father to Henny.

Henny opened her mouth to say 'No', and as she did so, she felt the sharpest stab of pain yet. Here's a kind man offering to take this pain away, she thought, and you keep refusing his help, you old fool, you. Forget about 'What can't be cured must be endured'. How about 'Don't look a gift horse in the mouth'? Or rather, 'Don't stop a gift dentist looking in your mouth.'

'OK,' she said. 'I'll come. But I can't guarantee I won't run away again when I get to the door.'

'I don't think you will,' said George Good, and before he left the house, he wrote a note to his wife and sealed it in an envelope.

'Give this to Mary when she gets back, will you, Henny, please?' he said.

Mary (it read),
Henny is suffering from bad toothache and a fear of dentistry. I can see her at 3.30.
Don't let her rat on me. Escort her to the surgery, all of you, and shove her in. I'll do the rest.
    George

George was right, thought Henny as she climbed into bed that night. He didn't hurt me at all.

At three fifteen the others had arrived home from the beach, and Mary Good had read the note and then showed it to the rest while Henny was out of the room. Angela and Barney read it, and then Eleanor read it to Rosie (who couldn't read her father's handwriting) and to Rowley (who couldn't read).

At three twenty-five they all said, 'Are you ready, Henny?'

'Ready for what?' said Henny.

'For your appointment.'

'Oh, that. I don't think I'll bother.'

'We'll all come with you,' Mary Good said. 'Off we go.'

Even at the surgery door Henny had not given up all hope of escape. But when she turned round, it was to face a solid wall of six Goods.

'In you go,' said Mary, ringing the bell.

'There's nothing to worry about,' said Angela.

'Like I said, he's ever so gentle,' said Barney.

'And the chair's ever so comfy,' said Eleanor. 'It lets right down, like a bed.'

'And there's a nice big picture to look at, on the ceiling,' said Rosie.

'And there's music playing,' said Rowley. 'Old-fashioned stuff.'

Bach? wondered Henny. Brahms? Beethoven?

'What sort of music?' she asked.

'The Beatles,' said Rowley.

And then at that moment the surgery door was opened and there stood a smiling girl who said,

'Good afternoon, Miss Hickathrift,' and before Henny knew it, she was inside.

Lying in bed now in the little flat, Henny pinched her cheek and her lip which had both gone numb from the local anaesthetic, so that they felt fat and she thought she must be talking funnily. Now the numbness had all disappeared, and, much much more important, the beastly toothache had quite gone. Though the tooth was still there.

George had repaired it.

'Don't want you to lose any more than you already have,' he had said when he'd finished. 'We won't do anything else today but there's quite a bit that needs doing. If you don't mind, that is?'

And to her surprise Henny heard herself saying, 'No, I don't mind.' Once he'd done the injection, she thought now (and to be honest, I never even felt it), and when I found nothing was hurting me, I actually almost began to enjoy it. Lying back in that comfortable chair, looking up at that picture – of a beach, but not one like Saltmouth: a palm-fringed Caribbean beach of golden empty sands and brilliantly blue seas – and listening to 'Eleanor Rigby', and hearing George's deep voice rumbling on above me, telling me little stories about this and that and occasionally asking me a question which I couldn't answer with my mouth stuck open. I really believe I'm not scared of the dentist any more, at least not of this one.

He's a good dentist, he is.

And then she smiled and said out loud, 'He's a *Good* dentist!'

And then she went to sleep.

Chapter Six
Bombing

One evening when the children were all in bed and Henny had just said goodnight and gone off to climb the steps to the flat, Mary said to George, 'The month is up.'

'What month?' said George.

'Henny's trial month. Remember, you agreed we'd give it a try, see how it worked out?'

'I didn't agree anything,' said George. 'You bulldozed me into it.'

'Are you sorry?'

'No. It seems to be working out quite well. As long as you're happy about it, Mary?'

'I certainly am. She does such a lot, you know. All that silver- and brass-cleaning, and the mending, and she irons quite beautifully, oh, and a hundred and one other things she does without being asked. I've got so much spare time now that I'm actually thinking of starting an Open University degree course. I wonder how I ever managed without my housemaid. Though that's a silly thing to call her.'

'Home help?'

'Well, yes. Or companion, perhaps, because she's not any sort of a servant, she's become a friend. And I'm sure she's happy here. Not least thanks to you.'

'Me?'

'Yes. All that dental work you've done on her, now that she's not scared any more. What have you charged her for it?'

The dentist stroked his bald head, looking faintly embarrassed.

'Not a lot,' he said.

His wife smiled at him.

'Nothing, you mean,' she said.

'Well, she hasn't exactly got money to chuck about. She only has her pension, and then she has to pay you for her bed and board, though I don't know how much you charge her.'

The dentist's wife ran a hand through her fair hair. She looked just a trifle flustered.

'Not much,' she said.

Her husband grinned at her.

'Nothing, you mean,' he said.

'Well, she's had a lot of expenses lately. Clothes for example – I had to persuade her to replace that old coat and that tea-cosy hat, and she needed shoes and so on. And she's always spending money on the children, did you know? Angela tells me that she regularly buys them ice-creams at the beach café.'

The very first thing that Henny had done as soon as she was able to draw her pension again was to go to the café, to reclaim her wrist-watch.

'Do you remember me?' she said to the owner. 'I owe you some money.' And she put three pound coins on the counter.

'Indeed I do, madam,' said the owner, 'but don't forget, you paid a deposit.' And he handed her not just the watch but also one penny, that had been her sole worldly wealth when she first arrived in Saltmouth.

'Thank you,' said Henny. 'Look after the pennies, my mother used to say, and the pounds will look after themselves.'

'Are you staying much longer?' said the café owner.

'I hope so,' said Henny.

On that same evening that George and Mary Good had been discussing her, Henny was lying in bed in the flat, thinking, Goodness! I've been here at Ivy Cottage a month already! And what a lot has happened since I ran away from the Home. And how lucky I am to be living with this family and to have this lovely little room over the garage.

Before she turned out the light, Henny gave a last look around. On the door of the clothes-cupboard (in which were her new clothes) she had fixed, with Blu-Tack, things that the children had done for her. Angela had written her a poem.

> When we first set eyes on Henny
> She was seventy-five years old.
> All she had was just one penny,
> But she has a heart of gold.

Barney, his mind on his as yet unfinished Second World War project, had painted her a picture of battle. Better not do one of soldiers, he thought, seeing that her boyfriend got killed, so instead he had done a graphic and highly-coloured scene of a Lancaster bomber with strings of little bombs falling from it, while above it lots of Spitfires shot down lots of Messerschmitts in flames.

Eleanor and Rosie had done portraits of her.

Eleanor, who thought that Henny might be self-conscious about her height, had drawn a tall, thin old lady.

Rosie, who drew everyone the same, that is to say the same shape as herself, had drawn her short and fat.

The only similarity between the two portraits was that both were titled HENNY.

Hanging on the knob of the clothes-cupboard was Rowley's present, a long rope of seaweed.

'You can tell the weather by it,' he said.

'How?' asked Henny.

'If it stays damp and rubbery, then it's going to rain. And if it goes all dry and hard and crackly, then it will be fine.'

The seaweed had stayed damp, but the weather remained stubbornly fine.

Mary Good, who was a keen gardener, had given her a pot-plant.

'It's called *Crassula argentea*,' she had said, 'the jade tree. But some people call it the money-plant.'

'Perhaps I'll win the Lottery,' said Henny.

'Don't over-water it,' said Mary. 'It doesn't like that. And don't worry if it doesn't do well – I've got loads more of them.'

Now it stood in its heavy earthenware pot on the sill of the room's one window, which was directly over the garage door. Henny always slept with the curtains partly open, to let in a little light from the street-lamp outside, and with the window ajar, to let in the fresh sea-air.

She gave a last look at her poem, her three pictures, her seaweed and her plant. Then she took from her mouth what was the finest of her presents – from the seventh member of the Good family – a beautiful new set of false teeth, and popped them into a tooth-glass beside her bed, and turned out the light.

Henny had grown used to the occasional sounds of Saltmouth's late-night traffic passing Ivy Cottage, but the sound that woke her later was an unusual one. It was a kind of scraping sound, of metal upon metal, and it seemed to be coming from beneath her window.

Henny got out of bed and went quietly across the room and looked out. There, directly below, was a man, who seemed to be trying to open the garage door.

61

Her first thought was that it was George. But why would he want to get the car out at – she looked at her watch – two o'clock in the morning? She leaned out a little further and now could see by the light of the street-lamp that it was certainly not George.

George was big. This man was smallish.

George was bald. This man had a lot of hair, done in a pony-tail.

George had a key to his garage. This man, she could see, had some sort of crowbar in his hand with which he was trying, as quietly as he could, to force open the up-and-over door.

Some old ladies in Henny's position would have screamed or shouted for help, but all Henny felt was anger, anger on behalf of the Good family, *her* family, as she already felt it to be.

This nasty thief was actually trying to break in and steel their car, their beautiful big shining eight-seater monster (she had had a ride in it and so knew that it would take seven Goods and one Hickathrift).

What's more, he was trying to steal it right under her nose!

If I give a shout for George, she thought, the man will just run away. And I can't very well nip down the steps in my blue flannel nightgown

63

with the pattern of red roses, and grab him in a headlock. He may be small but I'm smaller and a heck of a sight older. Besides, he'd most likely knock my teeth out – the ones that aren't in the tooth-glass, I mean. What shall I do?

Then her eye fell upon Barney's painting of the bomber and then upon the money-plant at her elbow.

Quickly she picked up the heavy pot and held it out over the window-sill. Carefully, though her arms began to ache with the weight of it, she moved it fractionally this way and that – just like a bomb-aimer in a Lancaster – till it was, she judged, directly above that pony-tailed head below.

Then she dropped it.

Chapter Seven
Gambling

At breakfast next morning the children were told all about the bombing of the burglar.

'I was woken up by the sound of Henny shouting my name,' their father said, 'and when I got outside, there was this chap knocked out cold. I recognized him straight away, because he was lying on his back with his mouth open, and when I shone a torch on him I could see the repair work I'd done on his Upper Left Four. It was young Freddie Hooper – Hooper the boatman's eldest boy.'

'The one with the pony-tail, Dad?' asked Barney.

'Yes. He's been in trouble with the police before now.'

'Are you going to report him?' asked Angela.

'No, I don't think he'll try breaking into our garage again. He was so dazed he'd no idea what had happened – I told him it was part of our security system. Anyway, there wasn't any damage to the door worth speaking of, only to his head. He had a bump on it the size of a hen's egg.'

'Oh dear!' said Henny. 'And I broke your flower-pot too, Mary.'

'Don't worry,' said Mary. 'I've got loads of pots and lots more money-plants. I'll give you another for your room and then we need never worry about having the car pinched, thanks to the Patent Hickathrift Anti-Burglar Bomb.'

'We're very grateful to Henny,' said George to the rest. 'Aren't we?' And everyone cried 'Yes!'

and then they all clapped and then they sang, 'For she's a jolly good fellow!'

Henny looked round at the five red-headed children and their tall fair-haired mother and their big bald father, and thought what jolly Good fellows they all were.

After breakfast, when the dentist had left for his surgery, and the children for school, for the new term had started, Mary said, 'Well, Henny, the month is up.'

'What month?' said Henny.

'Your trial month. Remember, we agreed to give it a try, to see how it worked out?'

'Oh yes,' said Henny.

Oh no, she thought, don't tell me she's going to

say I've got to go! I couldn't bear to be a stray again.

'Well, what d'you think?' said Mary.

'Think?'

'I mean, is the work too much for you?'

'Oh no!'

'Are you happy with us?'

'Oh yes!'

'Well, that's all right then,' said Mary.

'I can stay?' said Henny.

'Couldn't manage without you. Did I tell you, I'm starting an Open University course? In French. We quite often go to France on holiday, it'll be useful – I hardly did any French when I was at school and George has got none, he just shouts slowly in English. Which reminds me, I must get myself a French dictionary. Oh, and I must go and find you another money-plant.'

'Talking of money,' Henny said, 'I haven't given you any, you know. I must pay for my bed and board, we agreed I should.'

'Don't worry about that,' said Mary. 'You more than earn your keep, with all the work you do. By the way, could you do a bit of shopping for me this morning? Nothing heavy.'

In the town, Henny collected the few little things on Mary's list. One of them was 'a National

Lottery ticket', and just for luck Henny got one for herself as well. Then she treated herself to a tube of fruit gums.

As she sucked one of these, held between her new teeth, she had a brainwave. I've got quite a lot of money now, she thought, because Mary won't take any, but she can't stop me buying her a present, and she made her way to a bookshop.

'Just look at this!' said Mary Good to her husband when he came home for lunch, and she put before him a very large new dictionary, on whose shiny cover was written

FRENCH – ENGLISH
ANGLAIS – FRANÇAIS

George picked it up and looked at the price on it and gave a whistle.

'Twenty quid!' he said. 'You've splashed out!'

'Look inside,' said his wife.

On the flyleaf was written:

To Mary Good
from Henrietta Hickathrift

Henny came into the room.

'How very generous of you, Henny,' said George, brandishing the heavy book.

'It's you two that are generous to me,' said Henny. 'I only wish there was some way I could repay you for your kindness.'

Perhaps I could win some money with this thing, she thought later. She was sitting on a seat outside Ivy Cottage, her Lottery ticket in her lap, watching the evening sun on the sea. I wonder what you have to do? The children will know.

The children were playing croquet on the lawn. It was a very special and difficult sort of croquet, because the slope meant that the croquet balls all tended to roll down towards the sea-wall, and anyway that's where the players tried to knock each other. It was also a dangerous game, Henny had found out on the one and only occasion on which she had played, because everyone bashed the croquet balls as hard as they could and your ankles were in great peril.

When the game was finished, four of them came up the lawn towards her, red heads bright in the evening sun.

Barney was grinning because he had won.

Angela was smiling because she didn't mind not having won.

Eleanor and Rosie were quite happy because they never won anyway.

Behind them, Rowley was still playing, all by himself. He placed the ball right in front of each hoop and then knocked it through, the only way he ever scored anything.

'Tell me,' said Henny to the four older ones. 'Do you know how to do this Lottery thing?'

'I do,' said Angela. 'I've seen Mum do it. You have to choose six numbers between one and forty-nine – that costs you a pound. Then when it comes to the draw, if you've got the first six numbers that they call out, you can win an awful lot of money.'

Rowley arrived in time to hear this.

'Seventy million pounds,' he said. 'A man did.'

'Seven*teen* million,' the others said.

'I don't think I'd want to win that much,' Henny said. 'I wouldn't know what to do with it.'

'Give it to us,' said Rowley.

'I have to choose six, did you say?' asked Henny.

'Yes.'

'Well look, there's me and there's the five of you. Let's each pick a number. Start with the youngest. What number d'you want, Rowley?'

'Five,' said Rowley. 'Because I'm going to be, soon.'

Then the rest made a choice, in turn, and each time Henny made against the chosen number 'a clean vertical line with a biro', as the instructions said.

'There we are then,' she said at last. 'Five – Twenty-five – Thirty-one – Thirty-nine – Forty-four.'

'Six,' said Angela. 'You have to pick six numbers, Henny. What are you going to have?'

'Oh, I don't know. Let's see, I'll say thirteen.'

'That's unlucky,' said Rowley.

'Which is what I shall be, Rowley, you can bet your bottom dollar,' said Henny. 'I never win these sorts of things. Waste of a pound, really.'

Chapter Eight
Rescuing

When Saturday night came, they were all glued to the television to watch the draw for the Lottery.

'If you win,' said George Good to his wife, 'do I get half?'

'Certainly not,' she said. 'I paid for the ticket and I chose the numbers and I'm going to spend the millions.'

'We all chose Henny's numbers,' said Angela.

'I chose Five, Dad,' Rowley said. 'Did you choose Five, Mum?'

'No.'

'You should have,' said Rowley. 'It will come up, it will, I bet you my bottom dollar.'

And sure enough it did.

'Number Five!' read out the pretty girl on the television.

'Yes!' cried the four older children.

'Told you,' said Rowley.

But that was it.

All Mary's numbers were wrong, and of Henny's the only correct one was Rowley's Five.

'You'd better let me pick them all next time,' he said.

'I don't think I'll bother again,' said Henny, but even as she said it, she heard her mother's voice saying, 'If at first you don't succeed, try, try, try again!'

The next day they all went down to the beach together. Now, with the holiday-makers all gone, the sands were comparatively empty and the Goods' chosen place needed no KEP OUT notice to protect it. As an added bonus, the mid-September weather was still fine and the sea still fairly warm, and the family bathed.

'Who's for a nice long walk, right to the far end of the beach?' said George afterwards, and everyone was except Henny, who said she'd rather sit and watch the sea, and Rowley, who wanted to finish digging a large grave for a dead jellyfish he'd found.

'I'll look after him,' Henny said, so the others set off without him. Sitting comfortably in the sunshine, listening to the gentle hiss and slap of the waves and the cries of the gulls, Henny watched the walkers gradually growing smaller as they made their way along the beach towards the distant headland.

When they were no more than dots, she

opened a book, but after a while she felt her eyes grow heavy and found that she was reading the same sentence over and over again. She took off her spectacles and put them in their case, closed the book, and promptly went to sleep.

She was woken by the sound of a child's voice, yelling. It sounded like Rowley's. She looked around. The dead jellyfish lay in its now completed grave, waiting to be buried, but of Rowley there was no sign.

Scrambling hastily to her feet, Henny strained her eyes in the direction of the yells, which were coming from the sea. Her heart in her mouth, she hurried down the beach and saw, quite a little way out, out of his depth certainly, a small figure that splashed wildly and shouted loudly, in terror, it seemed to her. Every now and then the figure would disappear beneath the surface, to emerge again shouting and splashing even more frantically.

He's drowning! Henny thought. He's gone in without his armbands and he's gone out too far and he's drowning, and without hesitation she plunged out towards the boy.

'I'm coming, Rowley!' she called. 'Henny's coming!' and determinedly she waded on out until, up to her neck now, she grabbed hold of a flailing arm and began to drag the child shorewards.

'Let go of me! Leave me alone!' he kept shouting.

'It's all right, Rowley, it's all right!' panted Henny.

Not until she reached the shallows, breathless and soaked to the skin, did she find that, without her spectacles, she had made a slight mistake. Suddenly she heard an angry man's voice saying, 'What d'you think you're up to? Kindly let go of my son immediately!'

'Oh dear,' said Henny, peering at the strange child. 'I thought he was someone else and I thought he was drowning.'

'Drowning?' said the man. 'He swims like a fish!'

'But he was shouting and splashing.'

'Children do,' said the man, 'when they're allowed to enjoy themselves without interfering old ladies grabbing hold of them.'

'I'm sorry,' said Henny, dripping.

'Busybody!' said the man.

Henny trudged back up the beach until she was near enough to see that Rowley was just completing his work, patting down the little mound that now covered the body of the late lamented jellyfish. He looked up.

'You're wet,' he said.

Then there was a thudding of feet as the other Goods, returning from their walk, caught sight of the bedraggled Henny and came running.

'Henny!' they cried. 'Whatever's happened?'

Henny managed a smile.

'I heard a child calling,' she said. 'In the sea. I thought it was Rowley.'

'And you thought he was in trouble?' asked George.

'Yes.'

'And you went in to rescue him?' asked Mary.

'Yes. But it wasn't him. It was another little boy and he wasn't in trouble at all. I didn't have my specs on, you see.'

'But surely,' they said, 'Rowley was right here, beside you?'

'No, he wasn't. I dropped off to sleep, you see, and when I was woken – by a child yelling – I couldn't see him anywhere so I thought it was him in the sea.'

'It was terribly, terribly brave of you, Henny,' said Mary Good. 'And you're coming straight home with me now this minute.' And she put a big towel round Henny's shivering shoulders and led her away.

When they had gone, George Good said to his youngest child, 'If all this happened because Henny couldn't see you, Rowley, where were you then? Did you go off somewhere by yourself?'

'Only for a mo,' Rowley said. 'Henny was asleep. She didn't notice.'

'Where did you go then?'

'Into the cave.'

'Why?'

'I wanted to do a wee.'

Chapter Nine
Ailing

Next day it was plain that Henny was not at all well. Whether or not it was to do with her soaking, she developed a cough and said she felt achy, and Mary Good put her to bed in the flat and called a doctor.

'She's got a bit of a temperature,' he said afterwards. 'I'll give you a prescription for a course of antibiotics for her.'

In their different ways all the children felt Henny's absence.

Rowley missed her because he was the only one with whom she would play croquet – he could not hit as dangerously hard as the others – and also she let him have two shots to her one.

Eleanor and Rosie missed her because she used to read to them. Each was in fact a good reader, but it's very nice just to sit and listen to someone else, especially if they read well, with all the proper different voices, which Henny did.

Barney was no longer able to ask her questions about the Second World War. She couldn't of course tell him about the fighting, but she had lived in London during the Blitz and knew all about the bombs and the doodlebugs and the V2s. He hadn't liked to ask much about her boyfriend, but she had told him that he had been a guardsman, Matthew Strong by name, and that he had been killed in the landings at Salerno in Italy.

Angela, as the eldest, was best able to appreciate Henny's many skills, as a needlewoman, for example; her first effort at knitting a jersey was at a stage where she needed Henny's advice.

All five children – each in a particular way – felt the want of their friend. In some funny way she seemed to them to have lived at Ivy Cottage for ages.

'Unfortunately,' said Mary to her husband, 'as well as feeling ill, she's feeling guilty.'

'Guilty? About what?'

'About dropping off to sleep when she was meant to be minding Rowley.'

'But there was no harm done.'

'But there might have been, she keeps saying to me. "It might have been Rowley in the water and I might not have heard him in time." Anyway, I've got the doctor coming again today – I don't think these antibiotics are working. Her temperature is still sky high, and she's beginning to ramble a bit.

I listened outside the door just now and she was saying, "Matthew! Matthew! It's all right! Henny's coming!" Who could Matthew be? A relative? We don't even know if she has any relatives. What happens if . . .'

'If what?'

'If she gets worse, and we need to contact someone in her family?'

'Well,' said George. 'That Old People's Home she was in, they'd know, if anyone would. Do you have their number?'

'Yes.'

'Let's ring them then.'

So they did, and were told only that Henny had a sister in Birmingham, she had said so in a note that she had left.

The Goods then rang friends of theirs who lived in Birmingham, and asked them to look through the local telephone directory to see if there was a Hickathrift listed. There wasn't.

'Anyway,' said Mary, 'it could have been a married sister.'

'She'll have to be admitted to hospital,' said the doctor when he came. 'She has pneumonia, there's not much doubt about it. How old did you say she was?'

'Seventy-five.'

'Hm. Her heart's all right. We'll just have to see.'

The children stood watching in silence as the ambulance men manoeuvred the stretcher down the steps from the flat and loaded Henny into the ambulance for the trip to the Cottage Hospital. Her eyes were open, but she recognized none of them, it was plain, and as the stretcher passed them, she said again 'Matthew! It's Henny, I'm coming!'

As they watched the ambulance disappear, the children's father asked, 'Has she ever talked to any of you about someone called Matthew?'

'Yes, me, Dad,' said Barney.

'A brother, is he? A cousin perhaps?'

'No, her boyfriend was called Matthew. The one that got killed in the War, in 1943.'

In the afternoon Mary went to the hospital.

'How is she?' asked George when he arrived home from his surgery.

'Oh George, I don't much like the look of things. She didn't recognize me, and she's got this horrid cough. And her temperature hasn't come down – I looked at her chart. They're trying a different antibiotic now and putting it directly into a vein in her arm. Perhaps it was partly because the women in the beds on either side were large, but Henny just looked so *small*.'

The children came in from playing croquet.

'How's Henny?' they said. 'Is she better?'

'Well, no,' said Mary. 'I wouldn't say better. Not yet. But she's in the best place to get better. It's a very good little hospital. They'll put her right.'

At the hospital they had asked her for Henny's details.

'Name?'

'Henrietta Hickathrift.'

'Age?'

'Seventy-five.'

'Address?'

'She lives with us – Ivy Cottage, St Edmund's Street.'

'Next of kin?'

'None that we know of.'

'She's not related to you, Mrs Good?'

'No. Just a friend. I'll give you my phone number in case you need to contact me. I'll come to see her again tomorrow morning.'

For some reason the phone seemed to ring a lot in Ivy Cottage that evening, and Mary Good, sitting by it, picked it up each time hoping against hope that it would not be the hospital calling.

They won't bother to contact me if there's any improvement, she said to herself, only if she's worse, or if she has . . . and then she suddenly realized what a dreadful thing Henny's death would be for them all. Yet she had only been a part of their lives such a short time.

But the phone calls were all from family or friends, none of whom had ever set eyes on Henrietta Hickathrift.

By next day there was no change in Henny's condition. George, who visited at lunchtime, had a word with the consultant physician, who happened to be a friend with whom he played golf.

'What are her prospects, Charles?' he asked.

'Well,' said the consultant, 'it's a very nasty pneumonia, George, and her temperature is still very high. Trouble is, if we can't get it down soon, she may well start having fits, and that will not be funny. Is she some relative of yours?'

'No. She just turned up on our doorstep. She'd run away from home, an Old People's Home to be exact, and my children brought her to my house. They'd seen this notice that she'd written in the sand with her walking-stick – "I am a stray old woman." She's turned out to be a very remarkable old woman, and we've all become very fond of her. We've adopted her, I suppose you could say. I just hope to goodness you can pull her through, Charles.'

'The next couple of days will tell.'

That night the long spell of good weather finally broke and it rained from dusk to dawn. Next day, in Henny's bedroom, Rowley's rope of seaweed, which had remained damp and rubbery, had now turned dry and crackly, Mary saw as she was dusting that afternoon. She half wanted to throw the dead-looking stuff away, but then she thought, no, I can't, it's Henny's, she'd notice if it was gone when she comes back. If she comes back.

After tea, the four older children were doing their homework. The rain had stopped, and Rowley, wearing his wellies, was playing croquet on the lawn against himself. Deprived of Henny as an opponent, he had invented this new method where he played using two different croquet balls, red against blue, taking alternate shots. This way, he always won.

His game ended, he raised his mallet with a shout of triumph, and trudged back up the lawn just as his father arrived home.

'Dad,' he said. 'When's Henny coming out of that hospital?'

'Soon, I hope, Rowley,' George said. 'I'm going there this evening to see how she is.'

'Can I come with you?'

George Good considered. Angela and Barney, he knew, realized that Henny was dangerously ill, that she might possibly die; and even Eleanor and Rosie had some idea, he felt, of how serious things were.

Rowley, though, was simply waiting for her to come home, expecting her to come home, and it had never occurred to him that she might not. Should he take him in to see her? Then he might understand how ill she was. Maybe then it wouldn't be such a shock to him if she did die. Henny wouldn't know the boy of course, she hadn't known anybody for days now. But each of the other children had visited, just for a few moments. Only Rowley had not.

'All right,' he said. 'You can come with me.'

'How is Miss Hickathrift?' he said to the sister at the door of the ward. I don't want to walk in and find an empty bed, he thought.

'A little better, you'll be pleased to hear, Mr Good,' said the sister. 'Her temperature is down – only a point or so but that's what we want to see – and she's breathing more easily. She should be clearer in her mind now, too.'

'That's marvellous!' the dentist said.

'At the moment,' said the sister, 'she's sleeping peacefully, so it's probably best not to wake her.'

'We'll be as quiet as mice,' said George. 'Won't we, Rowley?'

Rowley nodded.

They sat silently beside Henny's bed, and George, looking at her, thought, not for the first time, that he had seldom seen such an open, friendly and patently honest face as hers. Her mouth was slightly open as she slept, and it was with satisfaction that George saw the glint of those new teeth. Once she's fit again, I'll do some more work on her, he thought. I don't think I've got the bite quite right.

Then it was that Rowley sneezed.

Henny opened her eyes.

'Bless you!' she said, and then, 'Why, it's Rowley! And George! I'm not dreaming, am I?'

'No,' said George. 'You've not been very well, Henny. But you're certainly looking better today.'

'How long have I been in this place?'

'Four days.'

Henny shook her head.

'I've been in such a muddle,' she said. 'All sorts of funny thoughts in my head.'

She put out a hand towards Rowley and he took it.

'Bong jooer,' he said.

'Before long,' said George, 'you'll be coming home with us, Henny.'

'Home,' said Henny softly.

'One of the things my mother is always saying,' said George, 'is "East, West, home's best."'

'Funny,' said Henny. 'My mother always said that too.'

She yawned.

'Oh, I'm tired,' she said.

'You go back to sleep,' said George. 'Mary will be in in the morning. We'll say goodbye for now.'

'Goodbye,' said Henny.

'O rev wah,' said Rowley.

Chapter Ten
Wishing

'Two things, George,' said the dentist's consultant friend when the time came for Henny to be discharged from the Cottage Hospital. 'One, your Miss Hickathrift will need some time to recover. She's had a nasty illness, it'll be at least a month before she feels fit to do much. And the second thing is, are you fit for a round of golf on Saturday?'

Back in Ivy Cottage, Henny did indeed feel a bit weak.

'It's as though I've been run over by a steamroller,' she said, and she was glad of a helping hand from Angela and Barney to get her up the wooden steps to the flat at each day's end.

Mary Good would not allow her to do any work harder than sewing on a button, and encouraged her to ask for her favourite things to eat and drink, 'To build up your strength,' she said.

'I remember,' said Henny, 'that when I was once ill as a child, my mother gave me beef-tea.'

'Beef-tea you shall have,' said Mary.

And George told her that Guinness was good for her, and that drinking port did wonders for invalids. He gave her the stout every lunchtime, and a glass of port each evening.

'You can just think of them as medicine, if you like,' he said.

'Nice medicine,' Henny said.

The consultant was right. Not until about a month after leaving hospital did Henny begin to feel her old self once again. Then one morning Mary found her busy cleaning the insides of all the windows.

'Don't overdo it, will you?' she said.

'It's you that's overdoing it,' said Henny. 'What with George and all the children to look after and me on top of all that lot. You've had no time even to start on your French course. You need a break. Get George to take you away.'

'Where to?' Mary said.

'France, of course. Have a couple of nights in Paris.'

Mary laughed.

'I do have five children, you know,' she said.

'Yes,' said Henny, 'and you've got me. Am I not to be trusted with the children?'

'Of course! But you've been ill –'

'– and now I'm better.'

Mary did put up some sort of resistance, but the thought of the delights of Paris undermined her defences. Anyway, George jumped at the idea (which Henny put to him behind his wife's back), and the children (encouraged by Henny) played their parts.

'Just think of you and Dad strolling down the Champs-Élysées,' said Angela to her mother.

'And going to the Louvre Museum,' said Barney.

'And climbing the Eiffel Tower,' said Eleanor.

'And drinking lots of wine,' said Rosie.

'And eating frogs' legs!' said Rowley. 'Tray bong!'

So it was that, during the half-term holiday, Henny and the five Good children had Ivy Cottage all to themselves.

'Are you sure you'll be all right?' George and Mary had said as they left. They had told their next-door neighbours that they would be away for two nights and that George had given Barney his whistle, with orders to blow it hard if there was any trouble.

'Like that chap with the pony-tail?' said Henny.

'Young Freddie Hooper, you mean?' said George. 'Oh, you won't need the Patent

Hickathrift Anti-Burglar Bomb, Henny. Freddie's in prison, doing six months for car theft.'

And remembering the money-plant reminded Mary to give Henny instructions about looking after all her other plants, and that reminded George to tell Henny where the fuse-box was in case the lights went wrong, and where the stop-tap was in case a pipe burst, and how to regulate the central heating, and so on and so forth, until Henny almost had to push them out of the door.

'Anyone would think you were going for two months,' she said. 'Go on, off with you, and have a lovely time.'

At the very last moment Mary said, 'Oh, I forgot to fill in my Lottery ticket. It's in the drawer in the kitchen table.'

'Too late now,' George said. 'We shall miss our train. Come on, the taxi's here.'

'Oh, Henny,' said Mary. 'You fill it in for me, will you? Just one board, that's all I do.'

She looked in her purse.

'Oh, I haven't got a pound, only notes.'

'I've got one,' Henny said. 'I'll see to it. Off you go.'

'Goodbye! Goodbye!' everyone called except Rowley who shouted, 'O rev wah!'

After the taxi had disappeared and the children

had gone back into the house, Henny stood for a moment outside Ivy Cottage wondering what Paris was like (for she had never in her life been abroad) and hoping that George and Mary would enjoy their break.

Then round the corner of the street came the sweep's van, with Mr Pobjoy, Saltmouth's chimney-sweep, at the wheel, his face, as usual, grimed with soot. When you saw a sweep, Henny remembered, you could have a wish. But you mustn't wish until you'd also seen a dog's tail, or it wouldn't work. As if by magic, a dog appeared from a side street, a dog with quite a long tail.

What a bit of luck, thought Henny, and then she said out loud, 'I wish that George and Mary Good have a really lovely time in Paris.'

The dog came nearer, nosing about on the pavement, and then Henny recognized it. It was the same thin collarless mongrel that she had seen on the sands on her very first afternoon in Salt-mouth. It's a stray, like me, she had thought then, and by the look of things, it still was.

Henny was sure it was the same animal, partly because of its colouring – it was black, with a white patch on its chest and one white forepaw – but mostly because she remembered it as being different from most dogs. Its ears were not like

most dogs' ears. One stuck up, one hung down. It had quite a lot of whippet in it, Henny thought, a bit of terrier perhaps, maybe a bit of Labrador.

Some mongrels are downright ugly, but this one was rather attractive. Or you could be, thought Henny, if someone looked after you properly and put some flesh on you (for under the black coat, the dog's ribs showed clearly).

Whether Henny would have done what she did next if George and Mary had still been at home is hard to tell. But in fact she nipped back into Ivy Cottage, went to the kitchen, and looked round for something, anything, to offer the hungry animal. Then she remembered. Yesterday they had had sausages and mash, and surprisingly, considering the Goods' good appetites, there had been one sausage left over. She took it from the fridge and hurried back to the front door.

The black dog was still in sight, though it had moved a little further up the street.

Henny whistled.

At the sound the dog looked round, one ear cocked, one drooping.

'Here!' called Henny. 'Look!' and she held out the sausage.

Cautiously the dog moved nearer, muzzle lifted to test the air.

'Poor old boy,' said Henny. 'You haven't just been starved, you've had a few kicks in your time, I reckon. But I won't hurt you. And this will do you good. It's one of Mr Braintree the butcher's very best pork sausages. Come on, it's all for you. A present from one stray to another.'

Drawn by the sight and smell of the food and lulled by the sound of a gentle friendly voice, the black mongrel forgot his fears and with a sudden movement snatched the prize from Henny's fingers. In two or three bites, he gulped it down, and his long thin tail began slowly to wag.

'Nice?' asked Henny and the tail wagged faster.

Henny, standing in the open doorway of the house that had become her home, looked at the homeless young dog and was tempted. 'While the cat's away,' she heard her mother say, 'the mice will play.' Let's just see if he will come inside, she thought – George and Mary need never know he did – and then I can at least find him a proper meal of something before he goes off to wander about the streets alone again.

The front door of Ivy Cottage had originally been the front door of the middle cottage in the row of three from which the present house had been made. Inside, there was a longish passage, with various rooms on either side of it, that led directly to a garden door at the rear of the house. This in turn led to the sloping lawn at the back.

Now, leaving the front door wide open, Henny walked along the passage, opened the garden door at the far end and left it so, and then sat down on the seat where she usually sat to watch the children play croquet. The hoops and mallets and balls had all been put away for the winter now, and the lawn was empty except for a couple of seagulls that were walking about on the grass, regarding Henny with cold yellow eyes.

Henny sat quite still, looking out over the seawall below. You silly old woman, she said to herself, did you really imagine he'd follow you, a total stranger?

But then suddenly the seagulls squawked and lifted hastily away off the lawn, and she felt a cold nose nuzzling her hand.

Chapter Eleven
Adopting

'Henny! Where are you?'

It was Angela's voice, coming from the passageway behind.

Henny put a reassuring hand on the black dog's narrow head.

'I'm out here – on the garden seat,' she replied.

'Someone left the front door wide open,' Angela was saying as she came out of the passage, 'so I shut –' and then abruptly she stopped both walking and talking as she saw what was sitting beside Henny and gazing up at her.

'Gently,' said Henny quietly over her shoulder. 'He's probably a bit nervous of people. I don't think he's been very well treated. Come to him slowly. Put your hand out for him to smell.'

Angela did as she was told, and the dog sniffed at her hand and then resumed his fixed stare at Henny.

Angela sat down on the seat, beside the two strays.

'Whose dog is he?' she said.

'I don't know,' Henny said. 'Nobody's, I think.'

Nobody's, I hope, she told herself, for the dog, it was already plain, had attached himself to her, and the feeling was mutual.

'What sort of dog is he?'

'Heinz,' Henny said.

'What's that mean?'

'Fifty-seven varieties. Which reminds me, I need some proper food for him. I don't want to go myself' (once he's back out on the street he might just push off, she thought) 'so could you pop down to the corner shop and get a tin of dogmeat? Take the money from my purse – it's in my bag, on the kitchen table.'

'OK.'

'Where are the others, by the way?'

'Barney's reading, the rest are playing a game.'

'Listen then, when you come back, tell them about this dog' (must give him a name, she thought) 'and get them to come out here – not all together, one at a time – to meet him.'

When Angela had gone, Henny sat stroking the black mongrel, trying to think what to call him. As he sat beside her, the sweep of his tail (on which she had wished) reminded her of seeing sooty Mr Pobjoy in his van.

Of course, that was the answer! Not 'Pobjoy',

that would be a silly name for a dog, but 'Sweep'!

Angela returned, tin in hand.

'Shall I go and open it?' she said.

'Not now,' said Henny. 'Later. Have you told the others yet?'

'No.'

'Well look, get some of those little cheesy biscuits out of the barrel in the dining-room. Get one for each of you, to offer to him. Come slowly, quietly, tell them – I don't want him scared.'

So in a little while the Good children came out of the garden door, one at a time, and went slowly and quietly up to the black dog and gave him a biscuit, first Angela, then Barney, then Eleanor, then Rosie. Last of all Rowley appeared but there was no biscuit in his hand.

'I thought so,' said Angela to Henny, and to Rowley she said, 'You've eaten it, haven't you? I knew you would. I've brought a spare one, here you are.'

'Here you are,' said Rowley to the dog. 'What's your name?'

'Sweep,' said Henny. 'He's called Sweep.'

'How d'you know?' said Barney.

'Because I just decided to call him that.'

'He's got funny ears, hasn't he?' said Eleanor.

'He's thin, isn't he?' said Rosie.

'He is,' said Henny. 'You'd better open that tin, Angela.'

Seldom can a tinful of dogmeat have disappeared so quickly into a dog. They all sat in a row on the garden seat, watching as Sweep threw the meat into himself in a series of convulsive jerks, and then licked the bowl into which Angela had put it until it shone.

When at last he raised his head, he looked round at the six faces watching him, with a sort of grin on his own, and wagged his thanks. Then he lay down, at Henny's feet.

'Whose dog is he?' asked Rosie.

'I don't know,' said Henny.

'Are you going to keep him?' asked Eleanor.

'I don't know.'

I'd like to, Henny thought, but what would George and Mary say? Anyway, he may belong to someone in the town, he may have a perfectly good home of his own. But she felt sure that whatever home he might once have had had not been a perfectly good one.

'He just walked in off the street, did he, Henny?' asked Angela.

'Yes. He followed me.'

'I think I've seen him before,' Barney said.

'There are quite a few dogs like him in the town, just roaming around. They don't seem to belong to anyone. They pick up scraps of food that people drop and they poke their noses into dust-bins and litter-bins. I saw one down by the harbour the other day – one of the boatmen was cleaning fish, and the dog was gobbling up the fish guts. I don't know where they go at nights.'

I know where this one's going to go tonight if I have my way, and that's on a rug at the foot of my bed, thought Henny.

'I bet,' said Barney, 'that if you put Sweep back out on the street, he'd just trot straight off up the town looking for food.'

'I bet he wouldn't,' said Henny.

'How much?'

'Ten p.'

'Done!' said Barney. 'Go on! Try it. I'll go up to my bedroom – it looks out over the street – and watch what happens.'

'We'll watch too!' cried the others, and off they all ran.

Barney's right, thought Henny unhappily as she got to her feet, this creature's a nomad, a wanderer, a dog of no fixed abode. Silly of me to think I could just adopt him.

'Come, Sweep,' she said with a sigh, and she

went in through the garden door and along the passage, the dog at her heels.

When she opened the front door of Ivy Cottage, he showed no sign of wanting to leave. Only when she stepped out on to the pavement, encouraging him to follow, did he do so. Then quickly, feeling very guilty, Henny hopped back inside the house and shut the door in his face.

She stood in the passage, listening. She heard a little whine. Then came the scratch of claws on the door. But then there was silence. For some time Henny stood there, but there was no further sound. He's gone, she thought. I should never have done that to him. I should have made sure he *didn't* get out, not until he was much more settled and sure of himself and of me. Now I've lost him.

Then she heard the children tumbling downstairs, Barney in the lead with a ten p piece in his hand which he thrust into Henny's.

'He's just sitting there, on the doorstep, waiting!' they cried.

'Shall I open the door?' said Angela, and as soon as she did, Sweep rushed in, making straight for Henny, waggling and wriggling his whole thin body in the joy of being reunited with her.

For the rest of that day he stuck to her like a limpet, following her from room to room as she went about the house. He was polite to the children, allowing them to stroke and pat him, but it was plain that it was Henny with whom he had fallen head over heels in love. When she had a bath that evening, he sat outside her bathroom door, and when later, after giving him a last run in the garden, she made her way to bed, Sweep was up that wooden stairway to the flat as though he'd climbed steps all his life.

'Goodnight, Sweep,' said Henny as she turned out her light, and thump, thump, thump went that long black tail on the bedroom floor.

Henny lay awake for a few moments, thinking about all that she'd done that day, in case she'd forgotten anything.

The house had been cleaned, the shopping done (including more tins of dogmeat), the children had been fed, the dog had been fed, the house was locked up for the night, Barney had George's whistle (and was half longing for an excuse to blow it, Henny thought).

What else? Mary's plants – yes, she'd checked them. Wait though! Mary's Lottery ticket in the kitchen drawer, she'd forgotten to fill it in. I'll do it first thing in the morning, Henny thought. But, like I said, it's just a waste of a pound. I don't know why I bothered to do it that other time, it's a million to one against winning anything in a sweepstake like that. *Sweep*stake! she thought. Black cats bring luck, perhaps black dogs do.

Chapter Twelve
Worrying

As soon as Henny got out of bed next morning, she opened the outside door of the flat for Sweep to run down the steps into the garden. Because the lawn was fenced at either side, there was no way he could get out except by leaping over the sea-wall (which would have been suicidal), should he wish to escape.

Henny was becoming more and more confident that this was the last thing he wanted to do, but, as she dressed, she decided that she must put the matter to the test.

She had no time before breakfast to fill in Mary's Lottery form, and so she stuffed it in her handbag.

After breakfast she said to Angela, 'Will you be all right if I go out for half an hour or so? Barney can help you look after the little ones.'

'Of course,' Angela said. 'What about Sweep?'

'I'm taking him with me,' said Henny.

'But you haven't got a collar and lead for him.'

'I shall buy them at the pet shop.'

The pet shop was at the far end of the main street in Saltmouth (and that'll be a good test, Henny thought, to see if he stays with me in spite of other people or other dogs).

She needn't have worried. He stayed as close as he could to her. Does he really need a collar and lead? thought Henny. Yes, of course he does – what if one of the children wanted to take him somewhere? Anyway, a dog should have a collar with its name on, and she bought him an elegant narrow red one with a lead to match.

'There! Isn't that smart!' she said as they set off again. Sweep seemed to think so. He stepped out jauntily by her side, and there were not a few people in the streets of Saltmouth that morning who smiled at the sight of the happy little old lady and her happy black dog.

When they reached the Esplanade, Henny sat down on a bench facing the sea and took off the dog's new collar. On the little brass disc that hung from it she carefully scratched SWEEP with the point of a nail-file.

'There you are,' she said to him, fitting the collar back on. 'Now I really feel you're mine. If George and Mary have no objections, that is, though I don't know what I shall do if they have. Even worse, someone might come up and say,

"Hey! What d'you think you're doing with my dog?" But somehow I don't think they will. Come on, let's walk right along to the end and back, and then we must go home.'

The houses on the Esplanade were all alike, all tall handsome Victorian buildings that had once belonged to wealthy Victorian families. Each carried a brass number on its door.

Though once they had all been private dwellings, probably the most desirable in the town for their nearness to the beach and their views of the sea, now, Henny noticed as they walked along, almost all of them had been turned into boarding-houses, each carrying a notice advertising its name. Not surprisingly, one was called 'Seaview', and there were also 'Balmoral' and 'Gulls' Nest', 'Welcome House' and 'Costa Brava', 'Green-gables' and 'Clifftops', and many, many more, serving the summer holiday trade.

When they reached the far end of the Esplanade, Henny noticed that the last house – the first in the rank, that is – was one of the ones still in private hands, with simply its number – One – on the door, and out of interest she counted, on her way back, just how many others had escaped being converted to boarding-houses.

When she once more reached the house at the end where she'd started, Number Forty-nine ('Gleneagles'), she found that the answer was six. Only six out of forty-nine, she thought, and then a sudden thought struck her. She took Mary's Lottery card out of her bag and looked at it. Yes! Each 'board' – A B C D E – had forty-nine numbers on it. And you had to pick six!

'Stranger things have happened, Sweep,' she said. 'Let's walk back to the other end once more.'

This time as they returned, she took a pen from her bag and marked on the Lottery card the numbers of the six that were *not* boarding-houses.

1 6 21 26 31 42

'As good a way of picking as any other, I dare say,' she told Sweep. 'We'll go into the super-market on the way home.'

Outside, there was a notice that said NO DOGS ALLOWED. GUIDE DOGS ONLY, but Henny, confident now of Sweep, tied his lead to a ring in the wall, and went in alone.

She handed the card, with that 'clean vertical line' through her six chosen numbers, and a pound coin to the girl behind the counter, who put it into a machine out of which it quickly popped again, and then gave Henny a ticket marked with her numbers.

'I've forgotten,' said Henny. 'What else do I have to do?'

'Put your name and address on the back,' the girl said.

So Henny, without thinking whose ticket it really was, wrote:

Henrietta Hickathrift
Ivy Cottage
St Edmund's Street
Saltmouth

As she had hoped and expected, Sweep was sitting quietly waiting for her, though he greeted her as though they'd been apart for months.

Back at Ivy Cottage, once the new red collar and lead had been admired, Angela said, 'Mum and Dad rang up while you were out.'

'Nothing wrong, I hope?' Henny said.

'No, just to say they'll be back tomorrow afternoon. They said they were having a really lovely time.'

That's what I wished, Henny thought.

'Anything else?' she asked.

'No. It was a very short call. I asked did they

117

want to speak to any of the others but they said no, they were in a hurry, they were just off to Fontainebleau.'

'Did you say anything about Sweep?' asked Henny.

'No, I didn't want to worry them.'

'Worry them? You mean they don't like dogs?'

'No, I'm only teasing, Henny,' Angela said. 'We used to have a dog when I was small and Barney was a baby, but it died, and since then we've never had another one. Mum's been too busy with all of us, I suppose.'

'But Angela, what do you think they'll say?' Henny asked. 'About Sweep, and about him sleeping in my room? I mean, I'll buy all his food, he won't cost them a penny, and he's a very clean dog by nature, I'm sure of that, and he's obviously going to be good with you children, and it isn't as though he is a big dog – he doesn't take up much room – and because he's got a smooth coat, he won't leave hairs everywhere, and I'll bet he'll be a good house dog – a dog's the best insurance against burglars. If I'd had Sweep when that chap with the pony-tail tried to break into the garage, he'd have barked and the man would have run away.'

She stopped, out of breath.

Angela giggled.

'What's funny?' said Henny.

'You are. Anyone would think that that dog was the most important person in your life.'

Henny looked up at Angela, already so much taller than her, and smiled.

'*One* of the most important people,' she said.

But the more Henny thought of it, the more she felt that she had not behaved at all well. She was meant to be acting responsibly while the children's parents were away, she was in charge, and what had she done? Only introduced a stray mongrel dog into their house, that's all. OK, so they'd owned a dog before so they weren't people who didn't like dogs. But if they'd wanted another, they'd have got one, wouldn't they? Whatever would they think when they arrived home to find that *she'd* got one in their absence?

Suppose they said she couldn't keep Sweep? She couldn't bear that, she'd already grown too fond of him. Henny tried to imagine herself saying 'If Sweep goes, I go!' But she couldn't bear that, she was much too fond of the Goods.

When George and Mary did arrive home the following afternoon, and four of their children had said 'Hello!' and one had said 'Bong jooer', they asked, 'Where's Henny?'

'In her room,' said Rowley, grinning in a mischievous sort of way.

His parents looked round and saw that the other children were all wearing rather sly secretive expressions.

'Why is she in her room?' asked their mother.

'She can't be ill,' said their father, 'or you wouldn't all be looking like Cheshire cats.'

'No, she isn't ill,' said Rosie.

'What then?'

'She's with her friend,' said Eleanor.

'What friend?'

'A sort of boyfriend, I suppose you could call him,' said Barney.

'A boyfriend? In her room?'

'She'll be here in a minute,' said Angela. 'She asked us to sort of prepare the way a bit before she introduced him to you. So you wouldn't be too shocked.'

George and Mary Good looked at one another in bewilderment.

Then the door opened and in came Henny and Sweep.

Already in the short time he'd lived at Ivy Cottage, good feeding had filled him out a little so that his ribs were not so prominent, and Henny had groomed his black coat till it shone, set off by the smart red collar round his neck.

'Sit,' said Henny, and he instantly obeyed.

Then before any of the three adults could say a word, a torrent of speech burst from the five children.

'He was a stray!'

'Like Henny!'

'And she rescued him!'

'And he's ever such a good dog!'

'And he's called Sweep!'

'And he sleeps in the flat!'

'And he's ever so clean!'

'And Henny bought him a collar and lead!'

'And she's going to buy all his food, she says, he won't cost you a penny!'

'And he's potty about her, you can see that!'

'And she's potty about him!'

George and Mary looked at each other again, and they smiled.

'Well, Henny,' said George, 'we're very grateful to you for looking after things. We've had a marvellous time, but it's great to be back with the family once more – all seven of you.'

'Seven?' said Angela.

'Yes. You and Barney and Eleanor and Rosie and Rowley and Henny and Sweep.'

Chapter Thirteen
Winning

What with Paris and Sweep, there was so much to talk about that it was not until the next day, a Saturday, that anyone remembered about the National Lottery.

'Oh, Henny,' said Mary as they all sat round the sitting-room fire after lunch. 'I forgot to ask – did you remember to fill in my Lottery card?'

'Oh yes,' said Henny, 'but I forgot to give you the ticket,' and she delved in her handbag and produced it.

'Thank you,' said Mary. 'I owe you a pound.'

'No, that's all right,' said Henny. 'Have it on me.'

'I wouldn't dream of it. Anyway, it's really the other way round now – you chose the numbers, so it's more your card than mine. But I insist on paying for it.'

'No, no,' said Henny. 'This is your ticket, it's got your name on it.'

Mary turned the ticket over.

'Actually,' she said, 'it's got yours, Henny.'

'Has it?' said Henny. 'Oh, I am silly. The girl in the shop said, "Put your name and address on the back," and I suppose that's what I did.'

'It seems to me, Mary,' said George, 'that the easiest way is just to leave things as they are. Why don't we say it's Henny's Lottery ticket this week, not yours. She paid for it, she chose the numbers, her name's on it.'

'Of course,' said Mary. 'That's much the best idea. Here, have the card back, Henny – *your* card.'

Henny took the Lottery card and stood up in front of the fireplace. She held the ticket before her in both hands and, looking hard at Mary, said, 'Promise me now, this minute, that if this ticket wins *any* money, you and I will share it between us. Or else I will tear it in bits and throw them on the fire!'

'Oh, don't do that!' all the children cried.

'Quick, Mary,' said Henny, and she made as if to rip the ticket across.

'All right, all right!' laughed Mary. 'I promise.'

'Saved by the bell,' said George. 'Tell us, Henny, what numbers have you chosen?'

Henny studied the ticket.

'One – Six – Twenty-one – Twenty-six – Thirty-one – Forty-two,' she said. 'One of them might

come up, with a bit of luck, like it did the only
other time I've tried, and even that one I didn't
choose – Rowley did.'

'You should have let me choose them all this
time,' Rowley said.

That afternoon Henny and all the children went
for a walk, with Sweep of course. As they went
along the Esplanade, Henny looked again at the
numbers of the six private houses. What a silly
way to choose, she thought. She didn't tell the
children.

Once they were on the sands, Henny let Sweep off his lead, and they soon found that his idea of fun was having a stick thrown for him to bring back. And how he could run! There wasn't much doubt of the whippet blood in his veins – he went like greased lightning. And when another dog – another Saltmouth stray by the look of it – came near to Henny and the children, Sweep's hackles rose and he began to growl fiercely, as if to say, 'This is my family and you can push off,' which the other dog did.

Back at Ivy Cottage they were all hungry, especially Sweep. Henny now fed him only once a day, but she knew that the children slipped him bits of food under the table, and she had already caught both George and Mary offering him titbits.

He had not objected when George had opened his mouth to inspect it.

'I'm no vet,' said the dentist, 'but I should say this was quite a young dog. He's got all his forty-two teeth, in good condition too.'

'Forty-two?' said Mary. 'That's one of your numbers in the Lottery, Henny, isn't it? Now we mustn't forget to watch the draw. Ten to eight. BBC 1.'

Sharp at ten to eight, the seven Goods and Henny and Sweep (who only took notice when a dog appeared in an advertisement on the TV, growling at it for daring to come into Ivy Cottage) sat watching the pretty blonde who would very soon be calling out the winning numbers. She was smiling, showing a lot of very white teeth.

'Nice set, that,' said George critically.

He patted Sweep's black head.

'She's only got thirty-two,' he said.

When all the razzmatazz was over and the machine was spinning, sending the coloured balls – white, blue, pink, green and yellow – dancing and jumping around, the starting button was pressed and the presenter said, 'The flashing amber lights tell you when the balls have been selected,' and then 'Here comes the first ball!' It was a pink one. 'Number Twenty-one!'

Henny looked at her ticket.

'Well, at least we've got one right,' she said.

'Here comes the second ball!' said the presenter, and, as a green ball came down, 'Number Thirty-One!'

The children crowded around behind Henny to see the ticket.

'Look!' they said. 'You've got that one right too!'

The third ball was a white one. 'Number Six!'

'Yes!' cried the children. 'You've got three, Henny!'

'You've won ten pounds,' said Mary.

Then down came another white ball. 'Number One!'

'Yes!' shouted the children.

'I can't believe it!' said Henny.

The fifth ball was a pink one. 'Number Twenty-six!'

The children yelled louder still.

'Don't tell me,' said George. 'She hasn't got that one too?'

'Yes!' they shouted. 'She's got all five so far!'

'What's the sixth one on the ticket?'

'Forty-two.'

And then down the tube came a yellow ball, and spun, and stopped.

'And the sixth ball,' said the presenter, 'is Number Forty-two!' and all the Goods went mad, whooping and cheering, while Henny's lucky dog barked and barked with excitement, showing all his forty-two teeth. There was so much noise in the room that they never heard the number of the last to be called, the bonus ball, nor did they hear the voice of the pretty blonde as she read out the six, now rearranged in numerical order:

$$1 - 6 - 21 - 26 - 31 - 42$$

Henny had got them all!

'You've won, Henny!' the children shouted. 'You've won the jackpot!'

'A share of it anyway,' said George. 'There may be other people who got all six right, you know.'

'We can find out,' Mary said. 'You can telephone and they'll tell you what the total jackpot is and how many people it is divided between. I've got the number somewhere. Here it is. Oh, George, you ring up, will you?'

George dialled the number and they all fell silent, listening.

'I understand,' George said, 'that you can tell me the total of the jackpot for this week's National Lottery?'

And then: 'I see. And how many winners were there?'

And then: 'I see. Thank you. Goodbye.'

'Well?' cried everyone. 'Well?'

'Good job you didn't tear up that ticket and chuck it on the fire, Henny,' said George. 'The arithmetic is easy. The total jackpot is ten million pounds and there were ten correct answers. Henny, you have just won a million pounds.'

'*We* have won a million pounds,' said Henny.

She went over to Mary and gave her a hug.

'You promised,' she said. 'Remember? It's £500,000 for each of us. Better than a poke in the eye with a blunt stick, as my mother used to say.'

Chapter Fourteen
Remembering

Winning a great deal of money is a good thing for some people, and for others it is a bad thing.

Some may spend wisely and save wisely. Others may not save at all, but instead spend madly – on new houses, new cars, expensive clothes, foreign holidays, on any and every luxury that they never enjoyed before but now can afford (they think).

There were some of this second sort, no doubt, among the other nine winners of that week's jackpot, but for the Ivy Cottage winners there was never any question of frittering the money away. George and Mary Good were comfortably off anyway, fortunate enough already to have most of the things they wanted in life, and when the claim had been made and the money paid, they invested it all, carefully, as a nest-egg that would in due course see them through their old age.

They had no wish to change their lifestyle. George went to work in his dental surgery as usual, and Mary kept house, but with plenty of time now – thanks to Henny's helping hands – to pursue her French language studies. Both had tried their hardest to persuade Henny that it was rightly all *her* money, the whole million pounds, but she was not to be moved.

'You promised to take half,' she said, 'and that's what you're getting.'

Henny herself had never had any money worth speaking of. She had never owned a cheque book or had an account with a building society, so she asked George's help in dealing with her £500,000. He introduced her to his bank manager, and between them they fixed matters up so that she need never worry about money again.

She did spend some, however. The very first cheque she wrote (the first she'd ever written in her life) was for quite a large sum as a gift to the Saltmouth Cottage Hospital.

And though the beach café was closed for the winter months, she found out the address of the owner, the man who had let her have three pounds worth of ice-cream for a penny, the whole of her worldly wealth. Who had sent it, he never found out, but a delivery van arrived at his door with a case of whisky ('From a Well-wisher').

So the months went by at Ivy Cottage, while in the bedroom of the flat Henny's money-plant grew, slowly but surely, as did the money in her new savings accounts.

That was really the only thing that worried Henny. Not only did she have this large amount of wealth, but it was sitting there getting larger. And I don't need it, she thought. I've got everything I want, here in my dear little room, with my dog, and my friends George and Mary, and their red-headed children of whom I have become so fond. What ought I to do with all these riches? What will happen to it all when I'm gone?

As usual, the voice of the late Mrs Hickathrift sounded in her head at that moment.

'Where there's a will, there's a way,' she heard her mother say.

A will, thought Henny. 'A Will!' she said, and next time she saw George, she asked him for the address of his solicitor.

'I want to make my Will,' she said.

Oh dear, thought George. He looked at her critically. She looks pretty good, he thought, considering she must be nearly seventy-six by now – she's been with us almost a year. I must say, she's got a mouthful of really good teeth now, even if most of them aren't her own.

'Are you ill, Henny?' he asked.

'No, George, I'm fine,' Henny said. 'It's just that I've never made a Will, so I think it would be wise.'

'Of course. Good idea.'

Henny never told him, or anyone, what were the contents of that Last Will and Testament of Henrietta Hickathrift. Only the solicitor knew that, after a sum of money had been set aside for funeral expenses ('We've all got to die some time!' Henny said to him cheerfully), this was what it said.

> I GIVE AND APPOINT all my estate of whatsoever kind and wheresoever situate and everything over which I have any disposing power by Will unto Angela, Barney, Eleanor, Rosie and Rowley Good, to be equally divided between them as and when each attains the age of eighteen years.

'Rowley, the youngest, is five now,' she said to the solicitor, 'so that leaves him thirteen years to go. But with a bit of luck I might be around to see his eighteenth birthday. I'll only be just coming up to my eighty-ninth birthday.'

On her seventy-sixth birthday that summer Henny had a lovely party at Ivy Cottage. Mary had made a beautiful birthday cake on which stood two little china figures she had found in a knick-knack shop – a little old lady and a black dog. Among many other things to eat there were prawn-and-mayonnaise sandwiches, and the biscuits were of course 'squashed flies'.

After tea George went back to his surgery to

finish off the day's work, and the children went
out on the lawn to play croquet.

'No,' said Mary firmly, 'you are *not* going to
help with the washing-up, Henny, it's your birthday. Think of it, a whole year since the children
brought you to the door! Now go on, off you go.
Why don't you take Sweep for a walk on the
beach, it's a lovely evening.'

So Henny fetched her walking-stick and
Sweep's lead, and they set off along the Esplanade and down the steps to the sands.

The sea was very calm, and they set off along
the water's edge where a great many seagulls
were standing about, which gave Sweep the
chance of some high-speed gull-chasing, good
fun for him since the birds waited till the last
minute before flying up out of his reach.

They went a long way across the sands, and by
the time they returned the incoming tide had
narrowed the beach and the holiday-makers had
all gone back up, to 'Seaview' and 'Balmoral' and
'Gleneagles' and all the other boarding-houses or
hotels in the town.

Henny paused, recalling what had happened
exactly one year ago.

'I'd just set eyes on you for the first time,' she
said to Sweep, 'and you were homeless, like me.

And then I wrote a message on the sand with my walking-stick, like this.'

When she had finished writing, she walked away, Sweep beside her, and climbed the long flight of steps that led to the Esplanade high above.

At the top she stopped to rest, leaning against the iron railings that flanked the road, and looking down to the sands below. This time there was no one else there to read what she had written on the sand in large letters.

It was the same as the message of a year ago but for one different word.

I AM A LUCKY OLD WOMAN

it read.

Then Henrietta Hickathrift and her black dog Sweep turned and set off for home, while on the sands below the gentle waves washed out her happy words.